# The Happiest Day

by Michael DeSanti

ISBN-10: 1-944134-02-6

ISBN-13: 978-1-944134-02-0

This book is dedicated to
my mom and dad,
my greatest teachers of love.

I cherish the day
that I heard of the Truth,
as I sat with the owl
on top of the roof.
The wise old owl,
who was king of the land,
said to me, "Boy,
put out your hand."

"If you would like,
I will give you the key,
but only if
you do something for me."
"Of course!" I shouted,
almost falling off the roof.
"Well then, little boy,
You must go find the Truth."

"But who will I ask?
And where will I go?"
"I'm sorry," said the owl,
"I really don't know.
But if you come back
with the Truth in your hand,
I will give you the key
to all of the land."

"But, great owl," I said,
"I don't know where to begin.
Perhaps do you think
you can give me a hint?"
He said, "Little boy,
have you heard of the way
that leads to the happiest,
happiest day?"
"No, I have not,"
I started to say.
"Then ask all those you meet
and see what they say."

The owl gave me a smile
and sent me on my way.

So I set out hoping
to come back king of the land
and show the great owl
the Truth in my hand.

"I'll find him the Truth,
I know it, he'll see.
Then the old owl
will give me the key."

Quickly I left
from ol' North Carolina
and sailed the blue sea
to the tip of China.

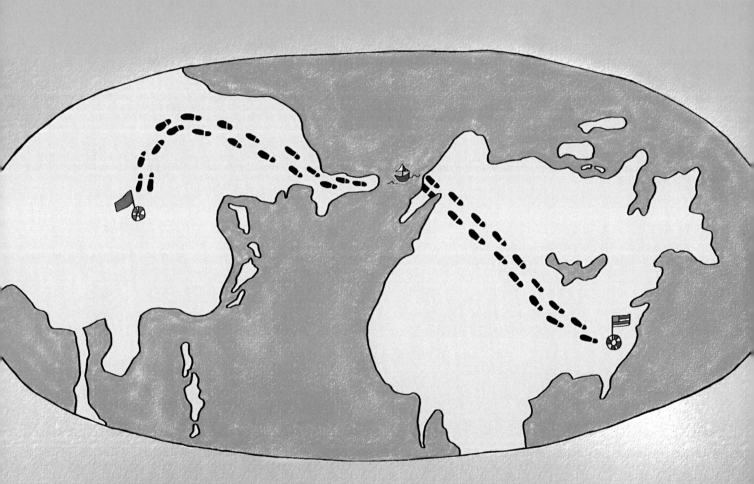

While on the boat I asked Skipper,
the captain of the sea,
"Do you think you can answer
one question for me?"

"Do you know the way
that leads to the happiest day?"

With anger he spoke,
"Little boy, can't you see?
I have no time for your games!"
He yelled back at me,
"Go back to your seat
and there you should stay."
Certainly, this man
knows not the way.

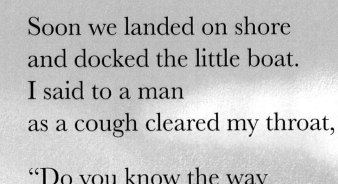

Soon we landed on shore
and docked the little boat.
I said to a man
as a cough cleared my throat,

"Do you know the way
that leads to the happiest day?"

"Little boy, are you lost?
Tell me, where did you start?
Is it a map that you need?
Or a graph or a chart?"
"No," I said softly,
"I thought you might know,
but I guess you do not,
so now I shall go."

Off to a city
I found my feet going,
to see if someone
was clever and knowing
of the way that leads
to the happiest day.

Down the sidewalk I walked
and entered a store,
where a man sat with bills
and papers galore.

"Do you know the way
that leads to the happiest day?"
He growled back at me,
"What's that you say?
Happy I'm not
with all these taxes to pay.
Please little boy,
get out of my way."

He pushed me aside
and out of the door
and screamed down at me,
"Don't come back anymore!"

On I went
in search of the way.
I had been gone one year,
one month, and a day.

While I was gone,
I grew quite alone.
I finally decided
it was time to go home.

Without the Truth, I came home.
So sad was I
that when I talked to the owl,
I started to cry.

I said to the owl,
"Oh, owl so wise,"
as tears filled my big,
baby brown eyes.

"I'm sorry!" I said,
with only air in my hand.
"I guess you shall stay
king of the land."

"Little boy, dry your eyes,"
the old owl spoke.
"There is one more place
you haven't yet looked."

"For to find the great Truth
and see it in your hand,
not a step should you take
from the place that you stand."

"And now," said the owl,
"You must close your eyes
if you would like to see
where the Truth lies."

So I closed my brown eyes
like the old owl said,
and suddenly the answer
came to my head!

"I've got it!" I yelled
and I screamed and I cried.
"The Truth's not out there.
The Truth is *inside*!"

I danced and I laughed
and I shouted with glee
when the wise old owl
asked the question to me.

"Do you know the way
that leads to the happiest day?"
I smiled at the owl.
"Yes," I did say.

I said, "To act out of love
to all things and to me."
Suddenly around
my neck was a key.

So now I cherish that day
on top of the roof.
The day that I realized
that *love* is the Truth.

# About the Author

Michael Desanti is a personal health and mindset coach. After reading The Lorax by Dr. Suess in school, Michael was inspired to create a book that teaches kids to live their own happiest days. So after school, at age 17, Michael penned his children's book, *The Happiest Day*, in just twenty minutes. His passion for supporting people to be the very best versions of themselves physically, mentally, emotionally, and spiritually continued into adulthood when he founded his health coaching practice, Authentic Self Healing, LLC. Michael works with clients all over the world. For more information, visit www.authenticselfhealing.com or www.michaeldesanti.com.

28095031R00021

Made in the USA
Middletown, DE
02 January 2016